THIS BOOK BELONGS TO

Mango Allsorts
Loving and level-headed;
Bambang's favourite medicine.

Guntur
Fluffy-eared cutie-pie; appearances may be deceptive.

Bambang
Curious and courageous; Mango's best flag-waver.

TEAM MANGO!

George
Conjurer of tapir transport; cricket *not* chess.

Minty Verbena
No introduction required; Hollywood's starriest star!

Rocket
Happy-go-lucky traveller; expert on fleas and doughnuts.

For Elliott, and all who were lucky enough to call him family, with love. P. F.

For Polly, with love. C. V.

First published 2016 by Walker Books Ltd
87 Vauxhall Walk, London SE11 5HJ

This edition published 2017

2 4 6 8 10 9 7 5 3 1

This book has been typeset in Veronan

Printed and bound in China

British Library Cataloguing in Publication Data:
a catalogue record for this book is available from the British Library

ISBN 978-1-4063-7341-7

www.walker.co.uk

Mango
&
BAMBANG
Tiny Tapir Trouble

POLLY FABER
CLARA VULLIAMY

WALKER
BOOKS

Contents

Seaside Rescue

Bambang stood in the middle of the sand, squidged his toes into the warm white grains and looked around happily. He'd never been to the beach before.

It was the very last day of Mango's summer holidays. New shoes had already been bought and pencils freshly sharpened. Mango's papa had decided that they should all have a proper treat in her last hours of freedom; a day out at the seaside for splashing and sunshine and (hopefully not *too* sandy) sandwiches.

Mango's papa settled himself on a deckchair under an umbrella and Mango changed into her swimsuit. The beach was dotted with groups of people sunbathing and playing games. Bambang, feeling rather proud of his jaunty new sunhat, went for a wander along the sand. He spotted an enormous castle being constructed by a family and trotted towards the shoreline to admire it more closely. A girl was adding turrets, while her father dug a deep moat and her brother stuck on shells and seaweed. It was very fancy. The smallest of the family sat near by, inside a large picnic cool box. He was pretending it was a boat and using his spade as an oar in the sand.

It was unfortunate that when the smallest of the family saw Bambang smiling at him, he burst into surprised tears. "MONSTA! PIGGY-MONSTA!" he wailed, pointing a stubby finger.

PIGGY-MONSTA! PIGGY-MONSTA!

His brother looked up. "What IS that, Dad?" he asked. The whole family stopped building and stared hard at Bambang.

"Don't know what it is, son. Could be something nasty washed in by the tide. Could have escaped from a zoo. Could be *dangerous*," said the father. He brandished his spade at Bambang in a threatening way. "Here you – shoo! You're scaring my family – get away from here! Go and find your own spot!" he shouted.

Poor Bambang turned away, his happiness quite gone. He tended to forget he didn't exactly belong. When people made him remember, it was a miserable feeling. It made him think of his brief time being stared at as an exhibit in Dr Cynthia Prickle-Posset's Museum of the Unusual. Bambang had been feeling quite relaxed since Dr Prickle-Posset had gone on the run. Now he shivered anxiously, wondering if he should always stay on his guard.

He took off his jaunty sunhat.

"I'm ready for you now, sea!"
Mango ran past him. She charged into
the waves. "Oooh! It's icy! Come on,
Bambang! What are you waiting for?
Bambang – what's wrong?"

Bambang was about to tell Mango
about the stares and the rudeness and
his sudden worry. He knew she would
make him feel better; even speak sternly
to the starers. But a bit of him couldn't
help thinking that maybe the family
were right. He *didn't* fit in here the same

way they did. He didn't quite match.

Bambang took a deep breath and found a smile for Mango. This was supposed to be her special day and he didn't want to spoil it. He ran to join her in the sea, shouting, "I'm coming now!" The cold water was a good distraction and before long he felt calmer again. The two of them had a wonderful swim; splashing and dunking and surfing to the shore on their tummies.

When they'd had enough, they lay
on their towels and let the sun dry them
off. Mango sat up and looked out to sea.
A motorboat was circling the bay, pulling
people on an attached parachute so
that they rose up and flew
above the water.

"Oh, look, Bambang! Wouldn't that be amazing? It would be like flying." Bambang did look. He felt doubtful. Tapirs didn't generally spend time dangling in mid-air and he felt there might be good reason for that.

"Ye-es," he said. "But perhaps those boats that keep you *on* the water would also be fun?" He pointed to a collection of pedalos tied up against a small wooden jetty.

"Oh, don't worry, Bambang. I wasn't really thinking *we* should go parasailing. But if you'd like to try a pedalo, I'm sure Papa wouldn't mind."

There were different sorts of pedalo. Mango and Bambang chose one in the shape of a flamingo. They set off to explore.

But the boat wasn't as easy to steer as they'd hoped. Bambang's legs turned out to not really be made for pedalling. Either Mango had to pedal by herself or Bambang had to do it with his snout. This made his bottom stick out awkwardly and he couldn't see where they were going.

"Why don't we just drift?" Mango suggested sensibly after struggling for a while. So they stopped pedalling and bobbed in the wide, calm blue. Mango had very brilliantly brought their picnic out on the boat with them, which meant they could eat it without getting it sandy at all. Bambang felt perfectly content.

They were washing the last mouthfuls down with lemonade when they heard a strange noise.

"Was that a seagull or somebody crying?" wondered Mango. They were too far from the shore for noises to reach them from there. She stood up and scanned the water. In the distance, some way out to sea, something was bobbing away.

"Oh, my goodness! Quick, Bambang! I think there IS somebody – look! There's a head sticking out of that box in the water!" Bambang looked and saw it was the smallest member of the rude family, the one who'd

WAAAH!

been startled by him earlier.
His pretend boat had somehow
floated out to sea. It didn't look
like it would *stay* floating for long.

Mango started pedalling furiously, but the pedalo was as stubborn and as slow to move as ever. They both glanced back towards the shore. A crowd of people had gathered and they were all pointing and waving frantically. Bambang didn't hesitate. He launched himself into the water and swam out strongly.

"Oh, yes – hurry, Bambang!" called Mango. "You'll be quicker than me."

Water was lapping over the edges of the bobbing vessel as Bambang reached it. There was no doubt it was close to sinking. The toddler was already crying, but he started to yell properly, scarlet-faced, when he saw Bambang.

WAAAH!

"Oh, please don't cry! I don't mean
to be strange. I can't *help* being a tapir.
But I'm afraid we can't wait for a
different rescuer. You need help *now*,"
said Bambang, paddling alongside him.

A large swell was approaching; there
really was no time to lose. Bambang
stuck his snout over the edge of the box
as water crashed over both their heads.

The box was completely upended. It
sank swiftly below the surface. There
was an awful moment when Bambang
thought its passenger had sunk, too.
Then the wave ebbed away
and to Bambang's
relief he found
two pudgy
arms were
wrapped around
his snout and
clinging on.

Bambang was a very good swimmer, but swimming with somebody squeezing his nose turned out to be nearly impossible. He tried to kick, but he couldn't even tell which direction he should kick in. He couldn't really breathe or see. The toddler was holding on very

tightly, poking his fingers in Bambang's eyes and thrashing and screaming in a furious panic. Bambang started to panic, too. If he gave in to it, he knew everything would be over and they would both go under.

BOO-HOOO!

Through the roar of water and child,
a distant voice reached him. "Try to calm
him down, Bambang! I'm on my way!
Hold on – oh, *please* hold on! I'm coming!"
Mango was pedalling as fast as she could.
Hearing her voice gave Bambang an
idea. With the last bit of strength he
had, he began to sing.

The effect was magical. The toddler
stopped yelling and struggling and finally
wriggled onto Bambang's back. His little

hands relaxed, and Bambang could
at last take a proper breath again.
"Nice piggy song. *Not* monsta!" said
the small boy as Bambang sang an old
tapir lullaby. Bambang didn't have the
strength to correct him. They floated
together, exhausted.

"Oh, thank goodness!" said Mango, arriving on the pedalo. She scooped up the precious cargo from Bambang's back and helped the tapir heave himself on-board. The party struck out for shore.

When they reached the waiting crowd, Bambang was shivering and spluttering and Mango's legs could hardly make it out of the boat, so wobbly were they from all the

pedalling. But a hero's welcome awaited them. There were cheers and applause and big towels wrapped round them both. And, even better, two very large cones of ice cream with double flakes were pressed on them by Mango's papa. The toddler seemed perfectly cheerful and none the worse for his adventure. No longer frightened, he now didn't want to leave Bambang and snuggled into him happily.

His tearful father burst through the crowd and flung his arms around Bambang. "You saved my little boy's life! I only took my eye off him for a moment while we finished sculpting the battlements and a wave swept him right away. And I'm so very sorry," the man bowed his head, ashamed, "we were stupid and rude earlier. Thank you. Oh, *thank you*! My family will always be in debt to you and your … family." The man paused, looking from Bambang to Mango and then across to Mango's papa, as if uncertain that "family" was quite the right word. "Is there anything we can do for you? Anything at all?"

Bambang looked at Mango. He felt quite brave now. "Please don't mention it. We were lucky to be in the right place, that's all. But, since you ask, there might be something..."

Bambang checked the fastenings on his harness for the fifth time. "You're sure this won't come undone? You're sure this can take our weight?"

The lady driving the motorboat turned round and gave them a big thumbs-up. Bambang heard the engine start. The boat moved off and a great colourful parachute billowed out behind them and began to pull on his harness. Bambang shut his eyes.

WHOOOSH!

They were lifted off the boat and up, up into the air.

"YIPEEEEEEE!" shouted Mango.

"WOOOAAAAH-OOOOOOH-AAAAAAH!" Bambang found his tummy was doing a most peculiar somersault inside him. But after a minute or two, he stopped feeling pulled and lurched about and started feeling floaty and free instead.

"Oh, Bambang, this is LOVELY. Oh, do open your eyes and see. It's like flying, it really is!"

Bambang half opened one eye, shut it again quickly, and then risked opening it again very slowly. Nothing terrible happened. He opened the other eye, too. Mango was right. It *was* all lovely.

"I can see Papa! Hello Papa! He's back snoozing under his paper," said Mango. "And there's the little boy waving at us. Thank you! Thank you for the lovely treat!" Mango called down to the family. They pointed at Bambang once more, but this time it was friendly and excited pointing. "What did the man mean about being rude, Bambang? I forgot to ask earlier."

"It doesn't matter now," said Bambang, who found that it really didn't.

"Well, this is an extra phooey to all those silly people who confuse you with a pig," said Mango. "Because whatever trouble pigs might have with it, tapirs can not only swim and do very brave rescuing, but they can ALSO quite definitely fly!"

And, as he flew, Bambang remembered that *sometimes* being a little unusual was a very good thing to be.

Jungle in the City

"No thank you, Mango. No warm brownie for me. I'm not feeling very pudding-ish today."

Mango looked up in surprise from the bowls she had been preparing. "Really, Bambang?"

"Maybe later. In fact I think I might go and have a little lie-down. It's strange; all of a sudden everything has gone rather wibbly around the edges."

Mango studied her tapir friend carefully. On close inspection he looked a bit  saggy about the snout. And was it her imagination or were his black stripes looking paler than usual? She put her hand on his head.

 "Oh, Bambang! You feel hot. I think you might be coming down with something. Our day at the beach last week *was* rather tiring. Maybe you picked up a chill? Let's get you into bed right away."

Bambang shuffled slowly off to be tucked up with Mango's softest blanket and her hot-water bottle. Mango sat beside him and stroked the tapir-shaped hump of bedclothes he made. She could feel him trembling in a horrid, shivery way.

"I'll bring you a bowl of the nice spicy soup Papa always makes me when I'm poorly and we'll see what the doctor says."

Finding a doctor who specialised in tapir medicine in the busy city where Mango and Bambang lived proved tricky. Dr Blossom was round, cheery and no help at all.

"Ooh, you are in a poorly pickle, aren't you?" she said, chuckling, after taking Bambang's temperature and listening to his tummy with her stethoscope. "I've no *idea* what the matter is I'm afraid!"

"He's not really eating anything," said Mango. "Not even cake. That's very unusual for Bambang."

"I'd think he wouldn't fancy anything much with his snout so blocked up," said Dr Blossom. "A cold is never nice for the nose and look how much nose this funny fellow has!"

A-HA-HA-HAA-

Bambang let out a sneeze that showed
off exactly that. It was loud and powerful
enough to make Mango's shelf of
treasures rattle.

A-AAA-CHOOO!

-AA

"I don't like this cold at all," he said in a bunged-up voice. "Plus it should really be called a *hot*." Bambang threw his covers off into a big pile on the floor.

"Of course you don't, it's rotten," agreed Mango. "Is there nothing you can give him?" she asked Dr Blossom.

"Nothing!" said Dr Blossom, positively beaming. "I think neither my green medicine nor my pink medicine would be of *any* use to a tapir. He'll either get better by himself or he'll get worse, I suppose! Ah well, goodbye my dear – and good luck!"

Mango was left to nurse her tapir as best she could. She made him mugs of hot honey and lemon, read him stories and mopped

him with a damp flannel. Bambang
was not an easy patient. Being ill does
not bring out the best in anybody, and
Bambang didn't believe that he would
ever feel better again. He was very, *very*
sorry for himself.

He said things like, "Let a tiger come
and eat me, Mango. Cynthia Prickle-
Posset can come back and put me in her
museum. I don't mind any more. I am too

sick to mind." And, in sudden feverish terror, "Maybe I've been poisoned! Maybe it was Cynthia Prickle-Posset *in disguise* who made those apple dumplings at the café last week! Maybe I shall die and be displayed in a glass coffin!"

Mango removed anything scary from the bedside pile of books after that. She was always soothing and patient. She did have to leave her friend to go to school, however. Bambang had visitors to sit with him during the day; the ladies from his flamenco class formed a rota. They brought him large linen handkerchiefs with his name embroidered in the corners, a basket of exotic fruits and a selection of magazines. They were full of suggestions for possible cures, not all of which were entirely helpful. Mango struggled to remain polite when she came home to find Bambang having hot mustard pasted thickly onto his snout or being urged to "dance the fever away".

But even if she felt the answer did not lie in these remedies, as the days passed Mango got more and more worried. Bambang did *not* seem to be getting better. He hadn't eaten for days and was noticeably thinner. He didn't even have the energy to be cross about being ill any more.

Their friend George came for a visit. He had brought a large inflatable banana with him, which would normally have been just the sort of joke to make Bambang laugh. But he barely even glanced at it.

"It's all my fault," said Mango miserably. "He would never have gone parasailing after all that swimming if it hadn't been for me. I'm sure that's what's made him so horribly sick."

"Nonsense," said George. "You don't get ill from *doing* things, you get ill from viruses. It says so in my *Giant Atlas of the Human Body*."

"If only there was even a *normal* sized *Atlas of the Tapir Body*," said Mango. "Then we might know how to fix him."

George knelt down by Bambang and stroked him. "Poor old man. Weren't you ever ill as a small tapir? *Think* now. What helped then?"

Bambang's eyes were shut. It wasn't clear if he'd even heard George. Then he whispered something. Mango and George leant closer to listen.

"There was a tree. A very tall tree with a very fat trunk and a *very* nasty fruit. Mother used to make me eat it," Bambang said weakly.

Mango and George looked at each other. "There may not be an *Atlas of the Tapir Body*, but I bet there will be a *Rare Rainforest Tree Encyclopaedia* in the City Library," said Mango. "Stay with Bambang. I'm going to go there straight away. It's our best hope."

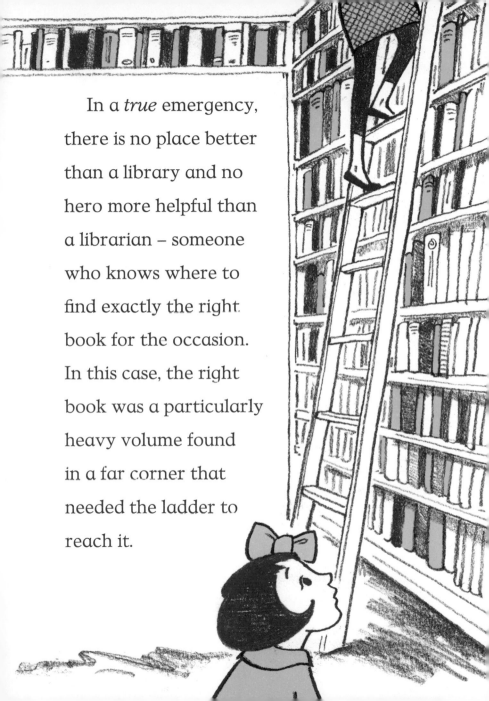

In a *true* emergency, there is no place better than a library and no hero more helpful than a librarian – someone who knows where to find exactly the right book for the occasion. In this case, the right book was a particularly heavy volume found in a far corner that needed the ladder to reach it.

The librarian passed it down to Mango and she sat at a desk, turning the pages anxiously until finally–

"'... very tall ... very fat ... *very* nasty fruit with medicinal applications...' The Boonanga tree! That's it! Oh, THANK YOU!" Mango hugged the librarian. The librarian looked pleased to be hugged. "I think I know where to find one, too," Mango continued. "But I'll need to work out how to move Bambang there..."

When Mango came home and explained her plan, George found the solution to this final problem. "A tapir ambulance? A few adjustments to my pull-along wagon should do it." They filled the wagon with cushions and blankets and painted a red cross and the words "Tapir Emergency Transport" on the side. Mango taped a large cup of blackcurrant squash with a curly straw to one corner, to encourage her tapir to drink.

Bambang groaned as Mango settled him in. She made sure he was wearing a warm hat and scarf in case of treacherous breezes and tucked him up lovingly.

Pulling the ambulance was hard work. Mango and George took it in turns, sometimes pushing as well.

There was one scary moment when the
pavement tilted downhill and they found
the weight of Bambang made the wagon
go faster than they'd intended.

"Excuse me, please! Poorly tapir coming
through! Mind out for the emergency tapir
ambulance!" shouted Mango, ringing a bell

TING!
TING!

TAPIR
EMERGENCY
TRANSPORT

as they raced to keep up. Pedestrians jumped to get out of the way, but thankfully no one's feet were run over.

Bambang had his eyes tightly shut and kept groaning. "This is far too bumpy. Where are you taking me?" he croaked.

"Here!" said Mango, stopping beside a sign that read "City Botanical Gardens". "We'll find what you need in the Tropical Zone Glasshouse!" They wheeled along a gravel path and pushed through the glasshouse's heavy wrought-iron and glass door.

A wave of steamy heat enveloped them. At first Mango couldn't see properly through the mist of warm water droplets, but as it cleared she found herself in a forest of green. Huge trees stretched up to brush the towering glass roof above. Long vines and enormous leaves of all shapes and shades hung over the central walkway.

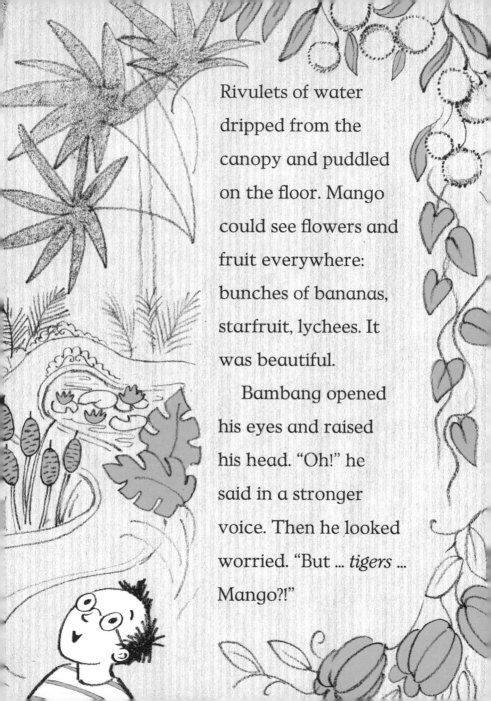

Rivulets of water dripped from the canopy and puddled on the floor. Mango could see flowers and fruit everywhere: bunches of bananas, starfruit, lychees. It was beautiful.

Bambang opened his eyes and raised his head. "Oh!" he said in a stronger voice. Then he looked worried. "But ... *tigers* ... Mango?!"

"No," said Mango firmly. "No tigers. It's just a *little* jungle, Bambang."

"Oh!" said Bambang again. "A little jungle in its own special house. I *see*." Slowly he emerged from his covers, pushed up to a sitting position and lifted his snout. For the first time since becoming poorly, he took a deep and easy breath without making any horrible snorty sounds.

"That sounds better. Of course," said Mango, "you needed a proper steaming! Now where's the Boonanga tree?"

"I'm checking the information boards," said George. "This way, I think..."

Mango and George pulled Bambang through the hot, damp greenness. In the middle of the glasshouse, where the roof was highest, they found the tallest and fattest-trunked tree of all.

"That's it!" said Mango. "That's the Boonanga!" They looked up into its branches. Fruit the size of footballs were growing right at the top. "Think we can climb it?"

"Looks tricky," said George doubtfully.

George and Mango were both very good at tree climbing, but the Boonanga tree proved impossible to grip. The bark was slippery, with no footholds at all. After many attempts, they collapsed at the bottom.

"It's no use," said Mango, rubbing angrily at her eyes where tears were pricking. "I'm sorry, Bambang. I've got you this far, but now I've let you down. I'm sure your mother would know what to do. I wish she was here for you. I seem to be no good at all... Bambang?"

Mango looked up to see her tapir wasn't listening. In fact, her tapir had gone. Bambang had apparently found the strength not only to get out of his ambulance, but also to disappear into the greenery.

Suddenly there was a great rustling and thundering from that greenery, then a rush of wind as Mango's tapir reappeared. He charged towards the Boonanga tree at tremendous speed.

"YAAAAAAAAAAR!" Bambang shouted. *THUNK* went his head against the base of the tree. *BOUNCE-BOUNCE-SPLAT* went a Boonanga fruit,

THUNK!

tumbling and ricocheting off branch and trunk before splitting open at Mango and George's feet.

"Wow!" said Mango, and then, *"Ew!"* She held her nose as the powerful smell of the Boonanga fruit was released.

"My nose cleared a bit and so did my head, and I remembered that tapirs don't climb trees," explained Bambang. "I remembered that we have other ways of getting fruit in an emergency."

"I'm so pleased!" said Mango. "Now *eat* the fruit. Your mother was right. I can already tell it will be very good for you."

Bambang nibbled a corner and pulled a face. "Perhaps I'll just stay ill," he said. Mango looked stern. He ate a bit more.

"It *is* unfair how the most powerful medicines are always the nastiest," said Mango.

She held her hand to Bambang's forehead. For the first time in days it felt a normal temperature. Mango slumped down on the tapir ambulance cushions, exhausted.

Bambang nuzzled her gently. "Thank you for making me better."

"I don't know that I did make you better, but I couldn't have *wanted* you to get better more. And I'm so very, very glad you are," said Mango, tears pricking again.

"You ALWAYS make me better," said Bambang firmly. He looked thoughtful. "Now the only bad thing I am feeling is a kind of horrible hollow rattling inside..."

"Ah. I think I might know how to get rid of *that* bad thing," said Mango, her confidence returning. "Could it be got rid of with buns in the

Botanical Gardens Café, do you think?"

"You see, you *do* know tapir medicine!" said Bambang. "How clever of you, I think it could!"

And it was.

A
Parcel
for
Bambang

Bambang's illness had taken a lot out of him. It would take time before he regained his full strength and a proper roundness to his tummy. He and Mango stayed at home more than usual, trying quiet things together. One evening they were getting to grips with learning origami, when there was a ring at the bell.

"I'll get that," said Mango.

DING-DONG

"Oh dear, all this folding is tricky, isn't it? Our swans don't look like the ones in the book." She opened the door.

"Parcel for Mr Bambang," said a delivery boy. He had a trolley with a big brown box on it. The box was covered with stamps and stickers. Mango signed his clipboard and the boy heaved the parcel off the trolley and into the middle of the room.

"How exciting!" said Mango. "Can you manage the knots, Bambang? It's quite a large parcel, isn't it? And ... is it a *squeaking* parcel?"

SQUEAK! SQUEAK!

FRAGILE

As Bambang ripped through the brown paper, the parcel did seem to be making a noise, and indeed shaking and rocking, in an unusual-for-a-parcel way. Before he could undo the last knot, the flaps at the top of the box burst open and Bambang's present revealed itself.

It was a tapir! A small one, still at the delightfully spotty stage. "Wotcha!" the tapir said. "Are you my big cousin Bambang? I'm Guntur. Pleased to meet you." Guntur hopped out of the box. He was very sweet. He had shiny black button eyes, fluffy-tipped ears and a small soft snout. He looked up at Mango and his eyes widened.

"And YOU must be Miss Mango. How pretty you are!" Guntur licked Mango's hand. "Thank you for unpacking me. It was a long trip in that box and Mum didn't put in *nearly* enough bananas." He looked expectant.

Mango recovered her manners and closed her gaping mouth. "A cousin of Bambang's come to visit? What a wonderful surprise! You must be very hungry if you travelled by post. Let me tell Papa you're here and see what I can find for you." She went into the kitchen.

"I didn't know I had a cousin!" said Bambang, still shocked. He recalled a rather domineering tapir from his past. "Is your mother ... my Aunt Wati, perhaps?"

"Yep, that's Mum," said Guntur.

He nosed around the apartment, then jumped onto the sofa Bambang often lay on and burrowed between the cushions. "She never mentioned you, either. But a monkey came by with an old newspaper clipping of you dancing. Mum *was* put out. She said she thought you'd been eaten by a tiger ages ago."

"There *was* a tiger..." began Bambang, but Guntur was still talking.

"Plus the parrots were squawking about a fierce lady marching through the jungle with a trap who was crazy-set on catching a tapir."

"Cynthia Prickle-Posset!" exclaimed Bambang, wide-eyed.

"I wasn't worried. Nothing scares ME. But Mum thought it would be best if I came to the city, too. She said if a tapir like you could make it here, I'd be sure to do *very* well," said Guntur. "I hope that girl hurries up with my snack. I'm starving."

He wriggled and stretched out on the sofa. Mango came out of the kitchen with a tray of toast, fruit, chocolate biscuits and a glass of milk.

"I'm sorry, we weren't expecting guests, but I hope there's something here you'll like," she said. "Are you planning a long visit?" Mango continued.

Guntur looked up, revealing a milk moustache and a mouth full of crumbs. "Oh, yes," he said happily. "I've come to live here now."

It became apparent over the next few
days that *two* tapirs in an apartment
were MUCH more than double one
tapir. After being in a parcel, Guntur
was full of energy. He spent the
nights snoring loudly in Mango's bed,
sandwiched between her and Bambang,
but from the moment he woke up he

ZZZZZZZ

was quite literally bouncing off the walls.
He did a lot of climbing up

and jumping on

and rearranging of things.

And, in Bambang's company, he did
a certain amount of *breaking* of things.
Guntur's attitude to the destruction was

airy: "They're a bit flimsy, those chairs, aren't they?" or "Well, THAT didn't work."

It was curious, but these breakages always happened when Mango was out of the room. When she came back in, Bambang would be sweeping up the mess, with Guntur sitting alone. Guntur, often wearing one of Bambang's hats, would look at Mango with a softly crinkled brow and say something like, "He doesn't always *fit*, my cousin, does he?" And then, "I love what you've done with your hair ribbon today, Miss Mango!"

And Bambang would watch Mango go pink and laugh.

There were other incidents outside
the apartment. It was true that nothing
scared Guntur; he courted attention in
a way quite unlike Bambang. He always
trotted proudly down the middle
of the pavement with his snout held

high. Passers-by smiled and stooped to stroke his silky back or tickle behind his ears. They said things like, "Oh, isn't he adorable?" and, "What a *cutie-pie*!"

And Bambang would watch Mango smile and nod.

One morning at the market, while Mango was occupied finding a ripe pineapple, Guntur pretended to be a watermelon on a fruit stall. He shouted "Boo!" at an old lady who tried to pick him up, then ran away giggling. The lady shrieked and fainted. Mango turned around in time to see *Bambang* bent over the lady's prostrate form. She rushed over to help.

BOO!

"Can I bring you one of these smoothies, Mango? They're quite as sweet as you!" called Guntur, somehow already on the far side of the market.

"Thank you, Guntur. That's very kind of you. I don't know quite what's happened, but I think this poor lady might need one, too," said Mango.

"Tee-hee! My cousin does seem to have a snout for trouble!" Guntur called back.

Later in the art gallery, while Mango puzzled over a picture of a very large rectangle with a very  small square inside, Guntur decided to play in the hole of a priceless modern-art sculpture in a different room. He got stuck. And it was Bambang who had to push him back through. So when Mango came in, she saw Bambang's

 head wedged in the sculpture, with an angry security guard pulling on his bottom.

"I did *tell* him not to touch," said Guntur, watching the tussle. He pushed his small, soft head under Mango's hand and snuggled against her side. Bambang, still being extracted from the sculpture, watched Mango run her hand down Guntur's back.

They were unceremoniously banished from the gallery. Bambang hung back a little on the pavement outside. He watched Guntur trot ahead with Mango, deep in conversation. Bambang felt his heart break. He knew what he had to do.

The next day Mango arranged a *very* fancy treat. "We'll take tea at the restaurant at the top of the Tall Tower! It revolves; you can see the whole city, Guntur."

A waiter brought a silver-tiered tray, laden with dainty sandwiches, scones and pastries, to their table. Guntur tucked in. Within minutes, the tray was nearly empty and Guntur's plate and mouth were full.

"Did you want one of those strawberry tarts, Bambang? Perhaps they can bring us more," said Mango.

"No," said Bambang, "I'm not hungry."
It was time. He looked out of the
window at the clouds and the tops of the
city buildings and took a deep breath.
"I've been thinking; now Guntur's here
and you two are having so much fun
together, maybe I'm making things a bit
crowded. I should go back–"

Bambang never got to finish his speech. Guntur had eaten a *lot* of sugar very quickly. He wasn't interested in looking out of the window at the view. Or in listening to Bambang. Or, for once, in sucking up to Mango. Guntur let out a loud hoot of joy, jumped down from his chair and went galloping off around the edge of the revolving circular room. His napkin, which Mango had tied round him earlier, billowed out behind him like a cape.

"Whoopee! Everybody watch me! I'm SUPER-TAPIR!" Guntur shouted. While he was looking back over his shoulder, he ran straight into a cake-carrying waiter. Waiter and cakes went flying. An egg-mayonnaise sandwich landed on the very avant-garde hat of a lady diner. The jazz band that had been playing suddenly found their instruments full of French fancies and éclairs. And this time Mango saw it *all*.

"GUNTUR! NO!" she shouted, then turned back and said more quietly, but with real anguish, "Bambang! No! How could you think I'd want you to go *anywhere*? YOU belong with me and Papa; not any other tapir. And I'm really NOT having fun with Guntur!"

Bambang looked startled. "Really? You're *not*?"

"No!" said Mango again, getting up from the table and going to help the waiters clear up the cakey mess. Bambang followed. "I was happy for you to have a real member of your family with you at last. I know how hard it is for you sometimes, being different. I've been trying to help Guntur feel welcome for *you*, Bambang."

"But," said Bambang, efficiently cleaning a custard slice off the floor, "I'm not nearly as cute as Guntur, or as brave as him, Mango. He thinks he's a much better tapir than me. He's not scared of tigers or Collectors. He says you just have to bite them on the nose. He even bit *me* on the nose to show me how."

"Did he? That's because he's never MET a real tiger or Collector," said Mango. "I'm so sorry to hear about your nose. I should have noticed more. Although I have been noticing some things. I think your cousin *might* be rather naughty, dearest Bambang."

"YES, he really IS!" said Bambang with relief. "I thought having relatives would be a nice thing, but it turns out it's all muddling and hard work."

"Oh, dear," said Mango. "Family muddles can be the hardest to smooth. We'd better go home and hope Guntur doesn't cause any more trouble today."

But, despite the egg-mayonnaise sandwich incident, Guntur was *not* in trouble. Super-Tapir was now on the lap of the very glamorous owner of the very avant-garde hat,  having his ears stroked.

"Gosh, that's Minty Verbena, the famous Hollywood actress!" Mango said. "I hope Guntur doesn't bite *her* on the nose, Bambang. It's a particularly expensive one." She went over.

"Darling!" exclaimed Minty Verbena when Mango coughed politely, introduced herself and indicated Guntur. "Is this darling *your* darling?"

"Sort of; he's staying with us. Actually he's *my* darling's cousin." Mango indicated Bambang. "I do hope he hasn't been bothering you. We'll take him home now. Come along, Guntur."

"But, darling!" Minty said. "We've just been having a marvellous chat! I want to keep the darling and he wants to stay with me too, don't you darling? Such charisma! He's a total poppet!"

"Miss Verbena is going to take me back to Hollywood and make me a star," said Guntur from Minty's lap. "She's much prettier and more important than you, and she'll love ME best. Because, whatever I do, *you* prefer Bambang."

He looked dismissively across at his cousin. "Which is very strange."

Minty popped a peeled lychee in the total poppet's mouth. "There are just NO tapirs in Hollywood, do you see, darling?" said Minty. "*This* darling is going to be ALL the rage."

It was not to be expected that everything could be sorted out there and then. As Guntur was a young tapir and under Mango's care, there were permissions to be sought and letters to be written to Aunt Wati, despite that young tapir's noisy tantrum and sulk.

But this time, as they left the restaurant with promises to be in touch with Miss Verbena soon, it was Mango and Bambang who walked together.

Guntur raced ahead, blowing raspberries and jumping in puddles.

Mango and Bambang didn't notice. There were so many conversations that they'd forgotten to have over the last week to catch up on. And, when Bambang tried to compliment Mango on her hair ribbon and she took it off and stuck it behind Bambang's ear, there was much relieved laughter to share.

Park
Games

Guntur's arrival in the busy city might have been makeshift, but his leaving was grand indeed. A fortnight after meeting Minty Verbena, Mango and Bambang waved him off to Hollywood at the airport. Guntur was carried onto the film star's private jet by his new personal assistant in a specially designed, velvet-lined travel basket.

There was a separate trolley for treats.

"Goodbye! Goodbye! Don't forget to write!" called Bambang. He'd got on much better with his cousin since he'd known Guntur was leaving.

"Oh, I shan't have time!" Guntur called back. "But you'll read about me in the papers and I'll make sure someone invites you to my first film première!"

"I think Guntur will enjoy being famous more than I did. He's better suited to it," said Bambang to Mango, as they went home to a suddenly much larger and quieter apartment. "But then he doesn't have you."

It was just as well the apartment was quiet. Mango had to concentrate. She was studying for the City Chess Tournament, which was held in the park each year. Although Bambang had never got to grips with chess himself, he was looking forward to going and supporting Mango. He knew he hadn't been the easiest company recently. While Mango practised, Bambang worked on an encouraging flamenco dance and made a Team Mango hat and flag.

On the day of the tournament, Mango queued with lots of other children and their families to register.

George was entering, too. "I shan't get anywhere," he said matter-of-factly to Mango and Bambang. "But I don't mind having a go, and then I can cheer you on when I get knocked out."

THE FINANCIAL HERALD
PRICE OF
PINEAPPLES
PLUMMETS

TEAM MANGO

CITY CHESS
TOURNAMENT
this way ⇨

Bambang noticed a thin, pale boy at the front of the queue. He was with a man who was whispering very intently in his ear. The boy had a book called *Extremely Advanced Chess Strategy*. He flicked through its pages as the man talked.

"Who's that?" asked Bambang. "He looks very serious."

"Oh, he IS very serious," said Mango. "That's Fitzroy Kidney. He's won the tournament for the last three years. His father coaches him. He doesn't really talk to the rest of us and I've never seen him smile, even when he wins."

The tournament began. Lines of tables were laid out in the sunshine and children

were paired up. The idea was that to start with each child played every contestant in a series of short games, gathering points that would determine the finalists later. Bambang tried to concentrate on what was happening. As well as his hat, he'd brought his flag to wave for Mango.

But Mango had to look at the chess board and think quite hard. After a while, Bambang decided that he might be an even *more* useful cheerleader if he bought them both a bag of hot doughnuts from the park stand.

It was while he
was carrying them
back that he noticed
a familiar tail and
pair of back legs sticking
out of a hole, digging furiously.

"Rocket? Rocket! Is that you?" called
Bambang. The back legs were joined by
a body, front legs and lastly a small head,
dragging an enormous grubby bone
from the hole. It *was* Rocket, Bambang's
best dog friend, last seen heading off

for adventures on an

ocean liner.

"Yes! It's me! I'm back! Hello, old friend. How are you? Did you miss me? I've had a splendid time. I've seen half the world and come home for a bit of a rest before I see the other half. I've got loads of stories to tell you! Oooh – have you got *doughnuts*?" Rocket abandoned

her bone and danced around Bambang, licking him thoroughly all over. The two friends sat down and got satisfyingly sugary and jammy together as they caught up on each other's news.

"A cousin? And gone to Hollywood you say? Well I never! Mind you, *I* didn't think much of Hollywood. Too much salad and not enough sausages, if you ask me. But each to their own. And how's your Mango?"

"She's wonderful," said Bambang. "She's over there playing chess. Oh! I think we'd better go and buy another bag of doughnuts. These ones were for her and seem to have disappeared."

Watching chess with someone to chat to, and wrestle or have a quick run around with, was more fun. Mango waved to them both when she could. Bambang looked at the scoreboard. She was doing well.

"I think, if she beats this girl, she'll have

CITY CHESS TOURNAMENT SCORES

FITZROY KIDNEY	⊎⊎ II
MANGO ALLSORTS	⊎⊎ I
AISHA BUFFETT	⊎⊎ I
COLIN COLLINS	⊎⊎ I
NANCY CASSAVA	⊎⊎
FRANKIE SCOTT	IIII
RAFI GARCIA	IIII
GEORGE HORNBEAM	III
POLLY FABER	O
CLARA VULLIAMY	O

enough points to go through to the final!" he said with excitement. Bambang tried to send his cleverest thoughts to Mango. Rocket nudged him with her nose.

"Look at that poor man over there. I know that feeling. He must have *terrible* fleas!"

Bambang looked. It was the man he'd seen in the queue earlier – Fitzroy Kidney's

father. He did seem very ill at ease.
He scratched one ankle and then the
other, pulled one of his ears, adjusted
his tie and then shook his left hand in
an irritable way.

Fitzroy, playing against an older boy, seemed distracted by his father's fidgets. His nervous eyes darted up to him constantly. But it didn't stop him winning. Fitzroy moved his bishop decisively and said, "Checkmate." His opponent slumped in his chair. Mr Kidney became still, made a fist and nodded at his son. Neither of them smiled.

"Odd," said Bambang.

"Very," said Rocket. "But look! Your girl's won too! She's through to the final with that Kidney boy." Mango was shaking hands with her opponent and looking quietly pleased. Bambang waved his flag very fast and Mango grinned at him.

George came bounding up. "Well, that's me done. Not really my game. I'm more

about the cricket." He produced a ball
from his pocket and rubbed it on his shorts.
"Fancy helping me bowl, Bambang?"

"Yes, please. I think Rocket would like to
help, too," said Bambang. George threw the
ball and Bambang and Rocket took turns
to catch it and bring it back. Mango came
over, looking nervous.

"I can't beat Fitzroy Kidney," she said.

"Of course you can beat him!" said Bambang loyally. "Me and Rocket think his dad's got fleas. He can't stand still at all. Would now be a good time for my encouraging dance?"

Mango pulled his ear affectionately. "It *can* be very hard to stay still during chess, can't it, Bambang?" she said, then looked pale. "I feel sick. I think an encouraging dance is just what I need."

"Have a doughnut, too. It will settle your stomach," advised Bambang.

The atmosphere for the final was tense. All the other chess tables were cleared away and a crowd gathered around

the finalists. Even Mango's papa had left his books and come to lend his support. He stayed in the background so as not to distract Mango. In contrast Mr Kidney was right in the front row, directly facing his son. Bambang and Rocket were next to him.

As the game got underway, Fitzroy took an early lead, capturing a key knight. Mango chewed her lip and stared at the board.

"Come on, you can do it!" whispered Bambang. He found he was also feeling nervous-sick, despite the stomach-settling doughnuts.

Mr Kidney seemed to be very itchy again. He wriggled and scratched and swatted bits of himself after every move.

"I can't bear to watch that man suffer," Rocket whispered to Bambang. "He needs to have a good roll in the mud. It's the

only thing that helps with fleas. There's a lovely cool puddle under that tree over there. Let me try to tell him." Rocket jumped up and started pulling at Mr Kidney's sleeve, making encouraging yips.

Now Mr Kidney swatted at Rocket instead, and tried to detach her from his jacket. "Get off me!

Shoo! SHOO!" he muttered angrily, but Rocket, determined to be helpful, held on, tugging him towards the tree.

Fitzroy, who had been about to move his queen, apparently changed his mind at the last minute. His hand wavered uncertainly over different pieces, before finally moving his knight. Mango looked surprised and immediately moved her own queen. "Check!" she said.

 Mr Kidney made a
strangled noise, got hold
of Rocket with both
of his hands and more
or less threw her off him,
before resuming his frantic scratching.
"Charming!" said Rocket, returning to
Bambang. "Some people just won't be
helped. Oh, well." But Bambang had been
caught by a sudden idea.

Bambang sidled closer to Mr Kidney.
Then he did something very daring
indeed. Something rather naughty.
Something almost Guntur-ish.

Bambang poked Mr Kidney sharply in
the side with his Go Mango flag.

"OW!" said Mr Kidney, bending over and rubbing the spot.

"Oops! Sorry," said Bambang.

Mr Kidney turned back to the game. "No! Not *that* piece, idiot boy!" he burst out as Fitzroy picked up his bishop. There was low murmuring among the other onlookers.

"Well, you're being very confusing! What piece DO you want me to move? Oh, I've had enough of your stupid 'system'," snapped Fitzroy. He moved the bishop anyway and stood up from the table. Mango moved her remaining knight–

"Checkmate!" she said in amazement.

There was uproar and a small tussle when Mr Kidney made as if to run away.

Rocket grabbed on to his trouser leg and held on. Bambang blocked his path until the tournament judge could get to him.

But it was Fitzroy himself who said, "Look for the book in his jacket pocket. It's all in there: his whole list of signals and strategies is stuck inside. He's made me do this for years and I've had enough. Who wants to win by cheating? I want to play my own game. See you on the cricket pitch next year!" Fitzroy addressed the last part to George. He produced a ball from his pocket and strode off into the park, throwing the ball high up into the air and catching it.

"But, Fitzroy! My son! What about everything we've worked towards!" Mr Kidney ran after him, chess crib-sheets scattering from his pockets as he went.

Mango, Bambang, George and Rocket walked through the park together. Mango's papa had gone on ahead to prepare a celebratory feast for everyone at home. Mango carried her enormous silver cup and smiled and smiled.

"I can't believe it," she said. "But this
cup is for all of us. I would never have
won it without your help. The right *sort*

of help, of course: the flag and the hat and the dance and all of you just being here. *You* were quite brilliant, Bambang! How did you know they were cheating?"

Bambang looked modest. "I didn't *know*," he admitted. "I suspected. I took a chance."

"That's because, whatever *other* tapirs may think, you are the bravest and cleverest of all. I'm so lucky you're part of my family," said Mango proudly.

Bambang stopped and looked at Mango. There was something he needed to ask her. "Do we count as a family, Mango? The man at the beach wasn't sure and neither am I. I mean, I know Guntur is my *real* family, but..."

Mango threw her arms round him. "You couldn't be *more* my family, Bambang."

Bambang leant into Mango.

Mango, who encouraged him and nursed him and was there for him on the good and the not-so-good days. He understood. Family had nothing to do with who you looked like, what you were good at or where you started out. It was about who you belonged with. Who made you feel most completely yourself, *even* if that self was sometimes sad or jealous or had a blocked-up snout.

"Good," said Bambang. "Because I like being *your* family best of anything."

"*Bleurgh*. Enough soppy stuff," said George. "Race you down that hill?" That seemed an excellent suggestion. And although there was *plenty* of cheating and a lot of eventual arguing about who was the winner, nobody minded in the least.

Because that's how families work.

Also in the
MANGO & BAMBANG series

The Not-a-Pig

Tapir All at Sea

Superstar Tapir

"All the elements of a classic"
Literary Review